Scorpions

BY ELIZABETH RAUM

AMICUS HIGH INTEREST · AMICUS INK

Amicus High Interest and Amicus Ink are imprints of Amicus
P.O. Box 1329, Mankato, MN 56002
www.amicuspublishing.us

Copyright © 2016 Amicus. International copyright reserved in all countries. No part of this book may be reproduced in any form without written permission from the publisher.

Library of Congress Cataloging-in-Publication Data
Raum, Elizabeth.
 Scorpions / by Elizabeth Raum.
    pages cm. – (Poisonous animals)
 Summary: "This photo-illustrated book for elementary readers describes the venomous scorpion. Readers learn how these desert animals use the stinger on their tails to defend against predators. Also explains the threat of these stings to humans and what to do when they are encountered"– Provided by publisher.
 "Amicus High Interest is an imprint of Amicus."
 Includes bibliographical references and index.
 ISBN 978-1-60753-788-5 (library binding)
 ISBN 978-1-60753-887-5 (ebook)
 ISBN 978-1-68152-039-1 (paperback)
 1. Scorpions–Juvenile literature. I. Title.
 QL458.7.R38 2016
 595.4'6–dc23

2014038741

Editor: Wendy Dieker
Series Designer: Kathleen Petelinsek
Book Designer: Heather Dreisbach
Photo Researcher: Derek Brown

Photo Credits: Maximilian Weinzierl / Alamy cover; Daniel Heuclin / Nature Picture Library 5; Wayne Lynch / All Canada Photos / Corbis 6-7; NHPA / Superstock 9; Florian Schulz / Alamy 10; National Geographic Image Collection / Alamy 13; FLPA / Alamy 14; Ivan Kuzmin / Alamy 17; Mark Moffett / Minden Pictures / Corbis 18-19; Arterra Picture Library / Alamy 21; kavram / Shutterstock 22; Jim Zuckerman / Alamy 24-25; Janelle Lugge / Shutterstock 26; DK. Khattiya / Alamy 29

Printed in Malaysia

HC 10 9 8 7 6 5 4 3 2 1
PB 10 9 8 7 6 5 4 3 2 1

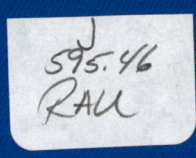

Table of Contents

A Deadly Sting	4
A Closer Look	12
Juicy Lunch	16
Staying Alive	20
Scorpions and People	27
Glossary	30
Read More	31
Websites	31
Index	32

A Deadly Sting

A scorpion crawls out of its burrow. Another scorpion passes by. It comes closer. They notice each other. They raise their tails. They attack! It's a fight. The big one flips the small one onto its back. Then the big one whips its tail. It stings. The sting is deadly. The small one dies. The big one eats it up. Yum!

**Two scorpions fight.
The loser will get stung!**

6

Scorpions don't like company. They use their killer sting to prove it. They sting one another. They sting **predators**. They sting people, too. A quick flick of the tail stings an enemy. The stinger at the end of the tail sends **venom**, a kind of poison, into the enemy.

The stinger on the scorpion's tail is called the **telson**.

There are more than 1,500 **species**, or kinds, of scorpions. Twenty-five species have venom that can kill humans. About 1.2 million people are stung each year. And 3,250 people die each year from stings. Scorpions kill ten times more people than snakes do. Mexico, Africa, and India report many deaths each year.

Q Should I worry about a deadly scorpion sting?

This black hairy thick-tailed scorpion lives in Africa. Its venom is very strong.

A Probably not. Only one deadly species lives in the United States. Only 4 people died in 11 years.

The striped bark scorpion is common in the southern United States and northern Mexico.

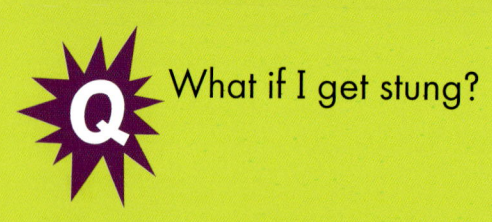

Q What if I get stung?

Scorpions sting when people step on them or touch them. People may not even see them. Most scorpions are less than 3 inches (8 cm) long. They hide in dark places. They hide beneath rocks or in piles of trash. In cities, they hide in cracks in the walls of houses.

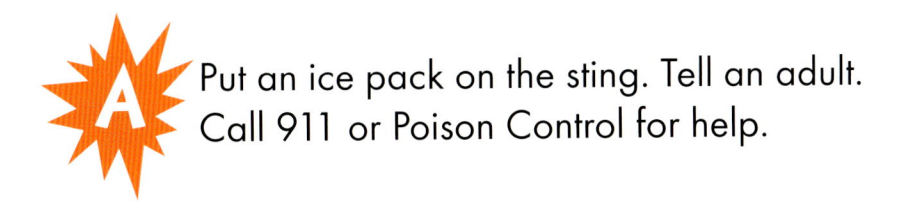

A Put an ice pack on the sting. Tell an adult. Call 911 or Poison Control for help.

A Closer Look

Scorpions are not insects. They belong to the spider family. Scorpions live all over the world. They do best in temperatures between 68 and 99 degrees Fahrenheit (20 and 37 degrees Celsius). They need soil to live. They dig underground. This keeps them cool on hot days. It keeps them warm on cold days.

Q Do many scorpions live in the United States?

Scorpions make burrows to protect themselves from extreme temperatures.

A Yes. About 75 species live in the United States. Most live in the deserts of the Southwest.

14

Scorpions have two eyes on top of their heads. They have 2 to 5 more along each side. The eyes see shapes and light and dark. But they don't see much with their eyes. They "see" with their legs. Tiny hairs on their legs and claws feel the air move. This warns them that something is nearby.

Look at the tiny hairs on this scorpion's legs. They help it feel when things are near.

Juicy Lunch

Scorpions hunt at night. They use their big claws, or **pedipalps**, to kill **prey**. They sit and wait. When an insect gets close, they strike! They raise their tails. They snap their claws closed. The strong claws trap the prey. They crush it. They don't sting to kill prey. They don't need to.

Q Why don't scorpions use venom when hunting?

This scorpion caught itself a cockroach.

A They save it to fight off enemies. It takes weeks to make new venom.

18

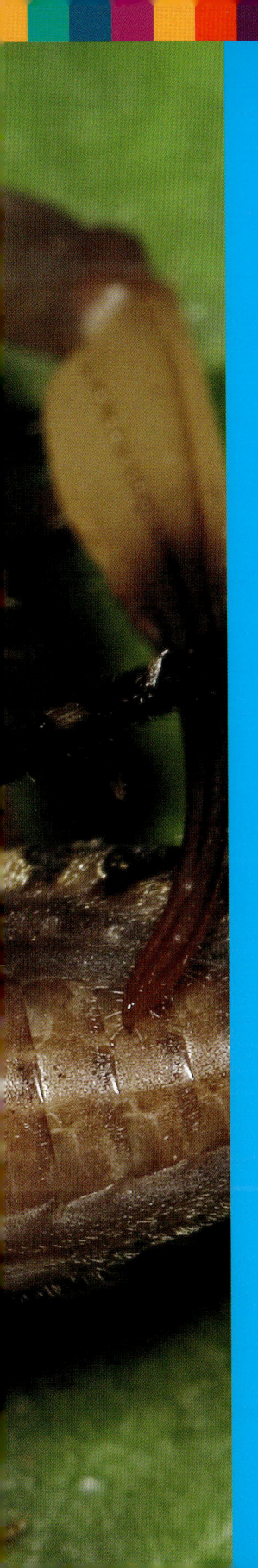

Scorpions tear the prey into bits with their strong jaws. They cover the bits with a special kind of spit. It turns the prey into juice. Then the scorpion sucks up the gooey mess. A big meal fills them up. They eat grubs, worms, and beetles. They eat grasshoppers. They even eat one another.

Scorpions use their claws to grab prey. Their jaws tear it up.

Staying Alive

Scorpions have many enemies. Snakes, lizards, and mice eat them. So do bats, owls, and other birds. Scorpions sting to deal with these enemies. They have two kinds of venom. One is weak. Scorpions use it on insects and small animals. It causes pain. They use stronger venom on bigger enemies. It can **paralyze** or kill.

A scorpion can make a good meal for a bird.

Scorpions live best in hot deserts.

Q How long do scorpions live?

Scorpions are tough. They can survive almost anything. They can live for a year without food. They can also survive in cold temperatures. One scientist froze some scorpions. Later, he put them in the sun. They thawed out and walked away. Some scorpions can live for up to two days underwater.

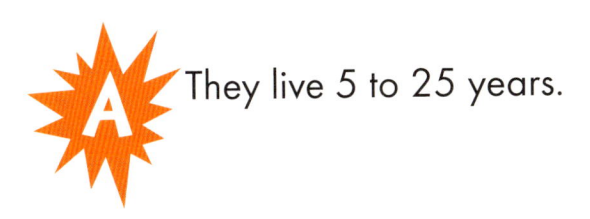

A They live 5 to 25 years.

On bright nights, the moon gives off **UV light**. We can't see UV light, but we can see how it makes scorpions glow. Why do they glow? No one knows. It may help scorpions find each other in the dark. But predators can find them, too. So the glowing may help a scorpion know to hide. Scientists are still learning why they glow.

A **black light** lets us see how scorpions glow.

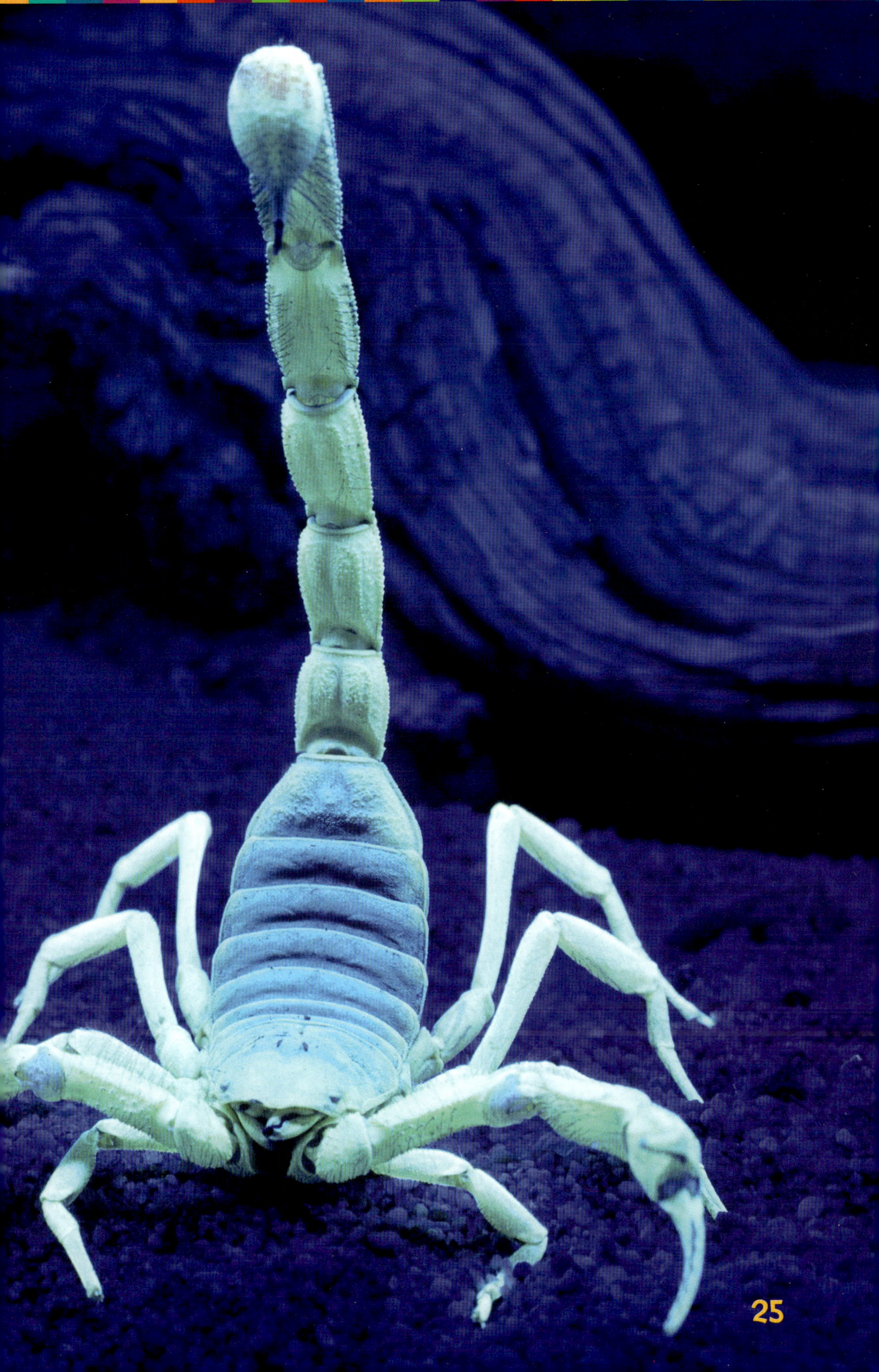

Mining can destroy burrows where scorpions live.

Scorpions and People

People fear scorpions. No one wants to get stung. So many people kill them. They hire pest control companies to kill them. Sometimes people destroy scorpion **habitats**, or homes. Some do it on purpose. Other times, it happens by accident. Farming and mining change the land. This can destroy scorpion habitats.

Some people like scorpions. They eat them. They remove the stingers and cook the scorpions. It's a fast-food treat in China.

In the future, scorpion venom may save lives. Doctors are studying it. It may help treat some kinds of cancer. It may help people with heart problems. Someday we may call scorpions "life savers."

Some people find scorpions quite tasty.

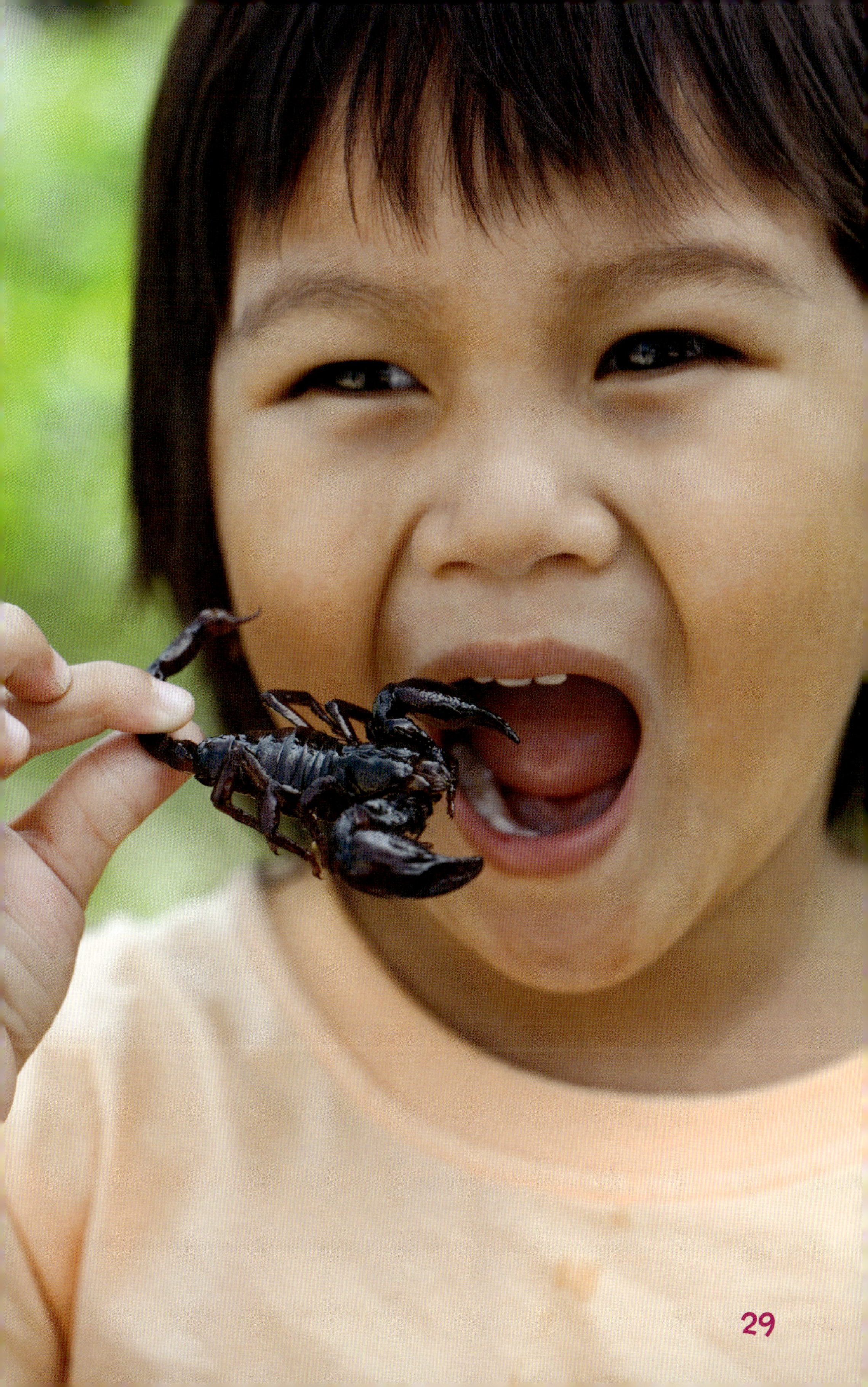

Glossary

black light A light that gives off UV light; scorpions glow under UV light.

habitat The place where an animal normally lives.

paralyze To make a person or animal unable to move or feel all or part of their body.

pedipalps The scorpion's claws or pincers.

predator An animal that hunts another for food.

prey An animal that is hunted for food.

species A kind or group of animals that share certain characteristics.

telson The end of a scorpion's tail where the stinger is.

UV light Short for ultraviolet light; light that is given off by the sun and moon; humans cannot see UV light.

venom Poison produced by some animals such as the scorpion.

Read More

Berger, Melvin. *101 Freaky Animals.* New York: Scholastic, 2010.

Markle, Sandra. *Scorpions: Armored Stingers.* Minneapolis: Lerner, 2011.

Otfinoski, Steven. *Scorpions.* New York: Marshall Cavindish Benchmark, 2012.

Websites

Animal Fact Sheet: Bark Scorpion | Arizona-Sonora Desert Museum
www.desertmuseum.org/kids/oz/long-fact-sheets/Bark%20Scorp.php

Anthropods: Scorpion | San Diego Zoo
animals.sandiegozoo.org/animals/scorpion

Hey! A Scorpion Stung Me! | KidsHealth
kidshealth.org/kid/ill_injure/bugs/scorpion.html

Every effort has been made to ensure that these websites are appropriate for children. However, because of the nature of the Internet, it is impossible to guarantee that these sites will remain active indefinitely or that their contents will not be altered.

Index

enemies 7, 17, 20
eyes 15
eyesight 15
freezing 23
habitat 11, 12, 27
hairs 15
hunting 16, 19
lifespan 22, 23
pedipalps 16
predators 7, 20, 24
prey 16, 19
size 11
sting 4, 7, 8, 11, 16, 20
stinger 7, 28
venom 7, 8, 16, 17, 20, 28

About the Author

Elizabeth Raum has worked as a teacher, librarian, and writer. She enjoyed doing research and learning about poisonous creatures, but she hopes never to find any of them near her house! Visit her website at www.elizabethraum.net.

5/23/16